Max Found Two Sticks

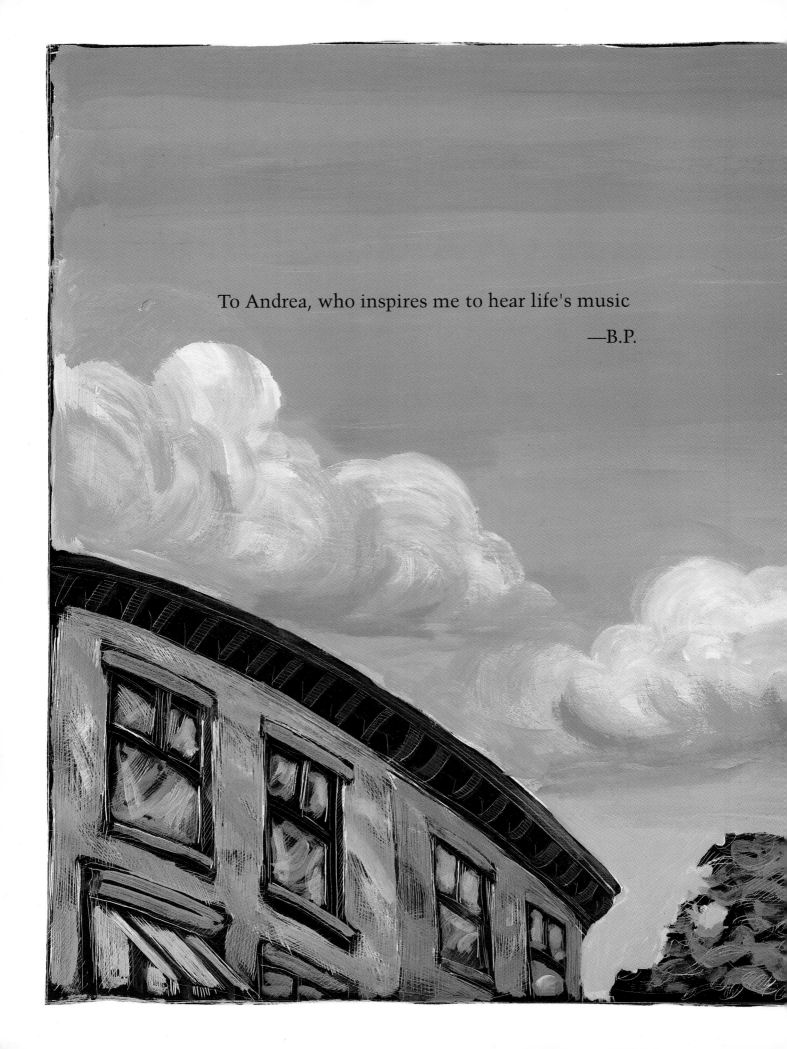

To Andrea, who inspires me to hear life's music

—B.P.

MAX FOUND TWO STICKS

BRIAN PINKNEY

ALADDIN PAPERBACKS

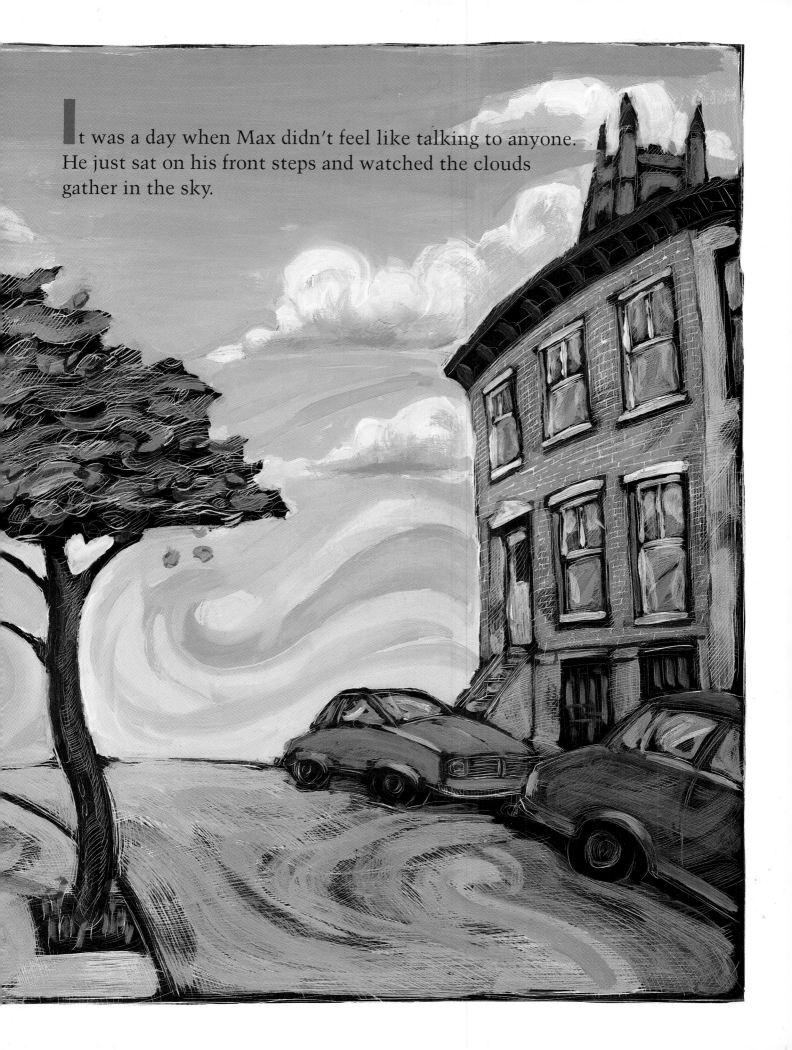

It was a day when Max didn't feel like talking to anyone. He just sat on his front steps and watched the clouds gather in the sky.

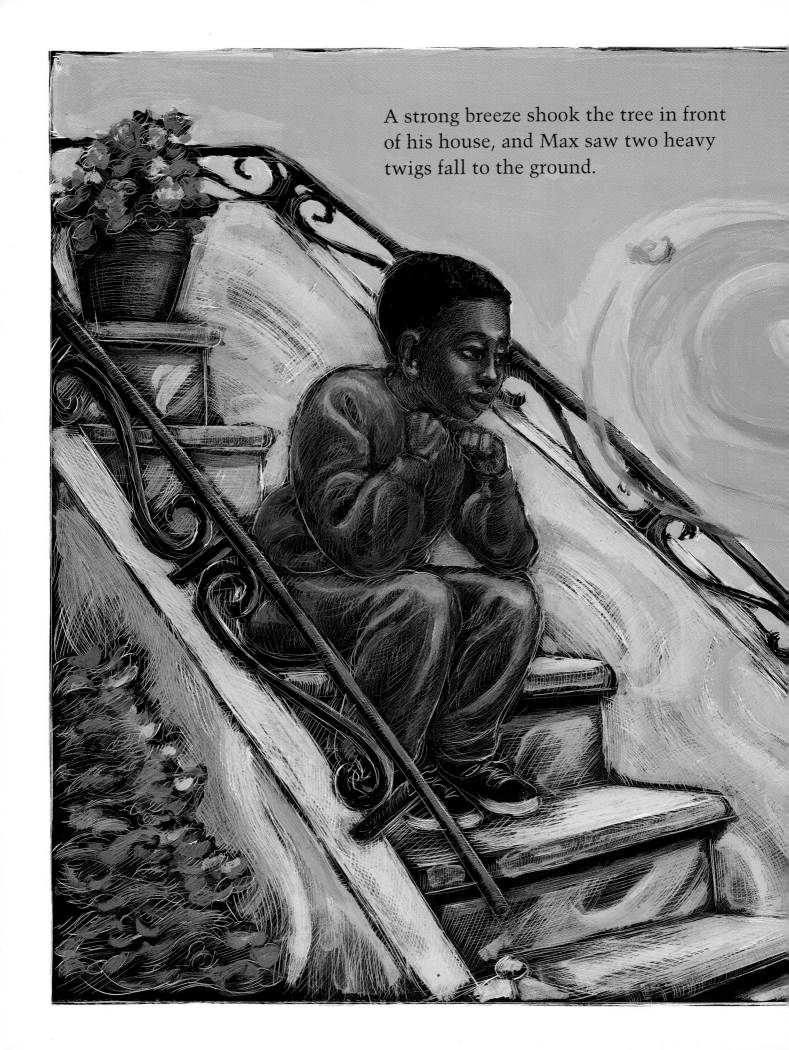

A strong breeze shook the tree in front
of his house, and Max saw two heavy
twigs fall to the ground.

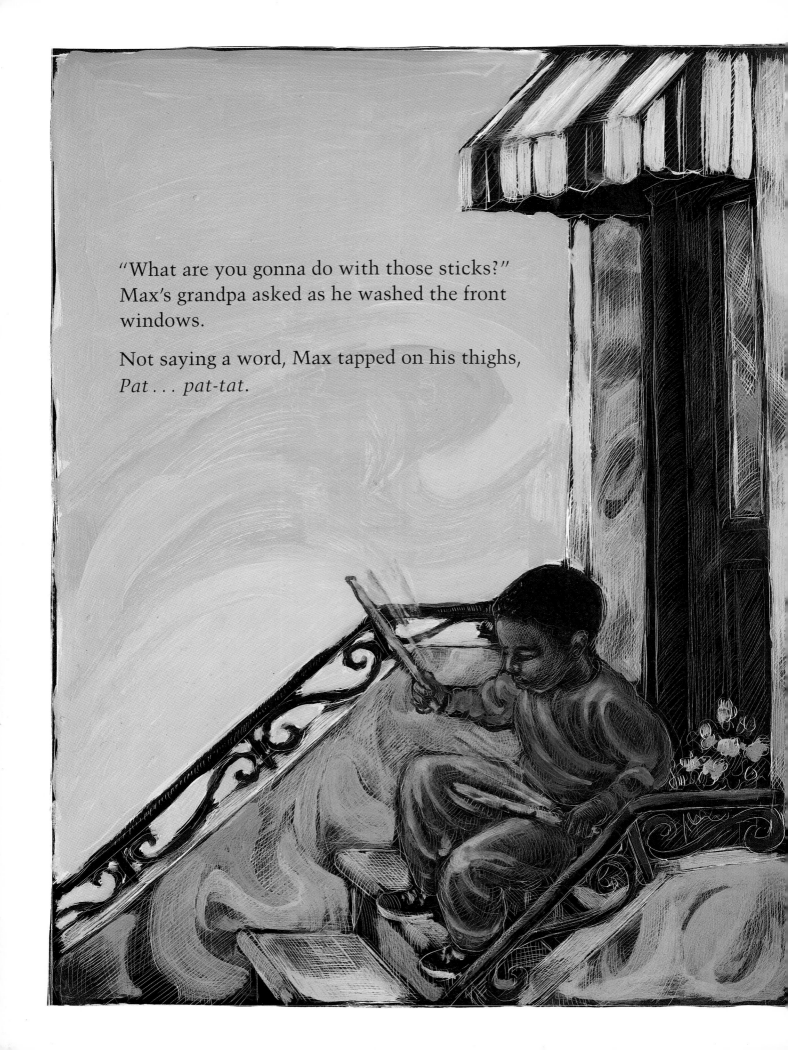

"What are you gonna do with those sticks?"
Max's grandpa asked as he washed the front
windows.

Not saying a word, Max tapped on his thighs,
Pat . . . pat-tat.

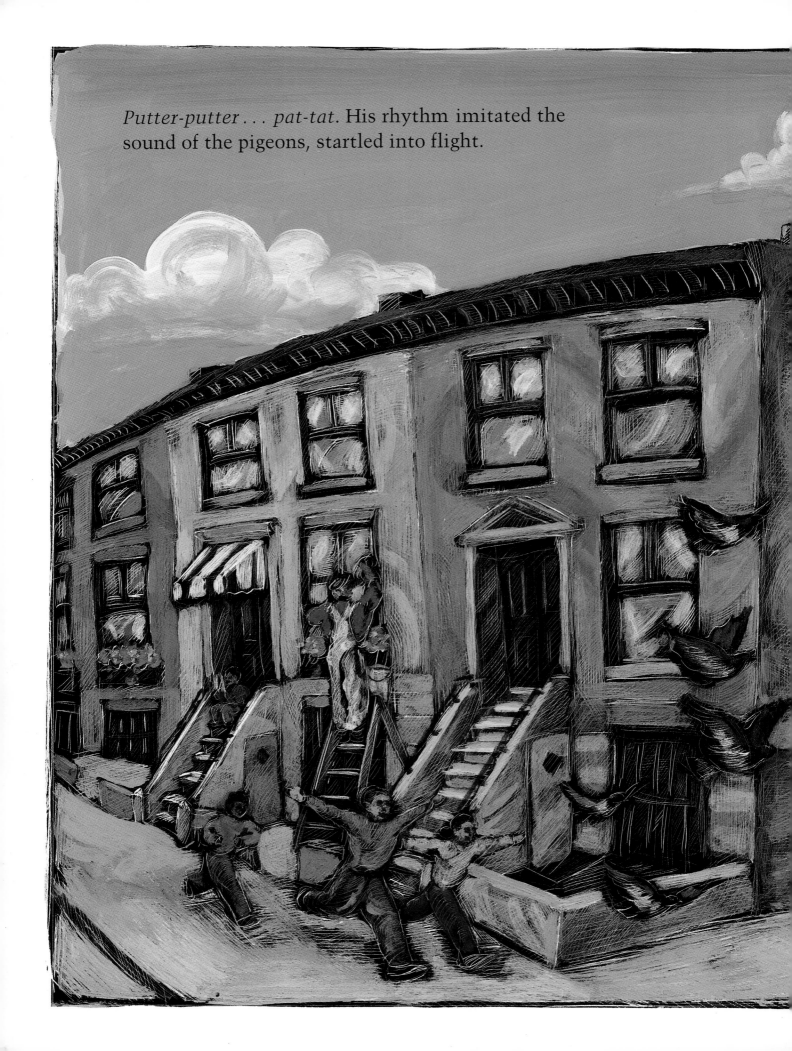

Putter-putter . . . pat-tat. His rhythm imitated the sound of the pigeons, startled into flight.

When Max's mother came home carrying new hats for his twin sisters, she asked, "What are you doing with Grandpa's cleaning bucket, Son?"

Max responded by patting the bucket, *Tap-tap-tap*.

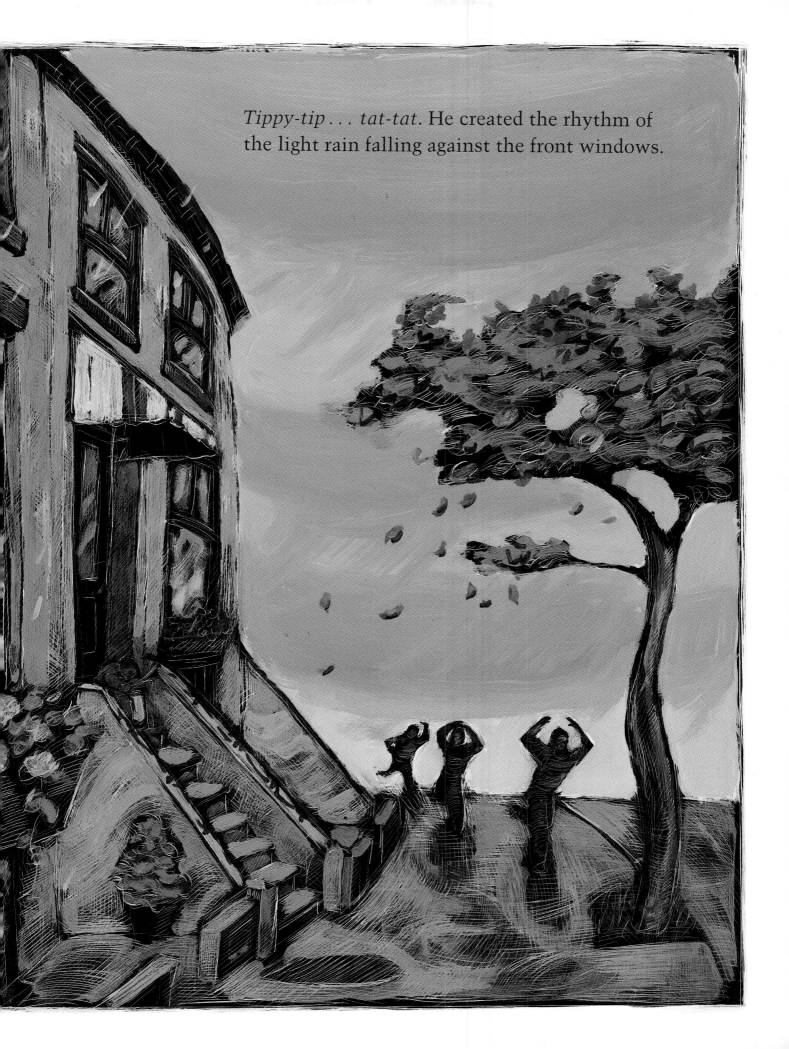

Tippy-tip . . . tat-tat. He created the rhythm of the light rain falling against the front windows.

After a while the clouds moved on and the sun appeared.
Cindy, Shaun and Jamal showed up drinking sodas.
"Hey, Max! Whatcha doin' with those hatboxes?"

Again Max didn't answer. He just played on the boxes,
Dum . . . dum-de-dum.

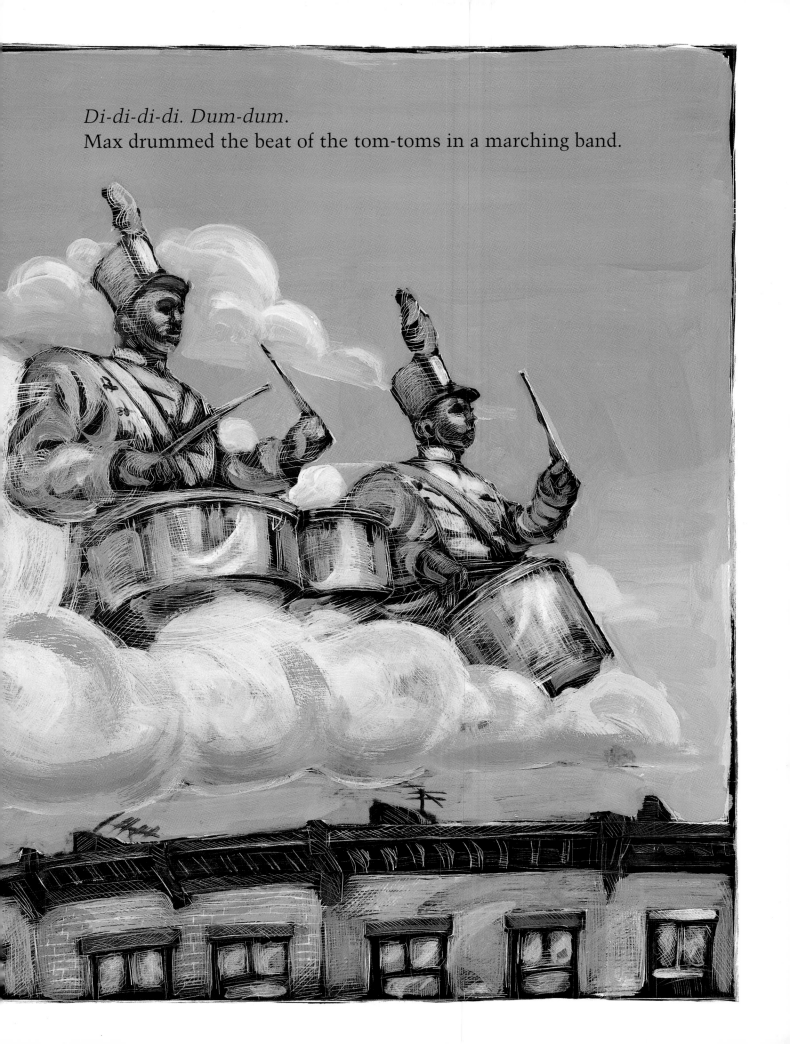

Di-di-di-di. Dum-dum.
Max drummed the beat of the tom-toms in a marching band.

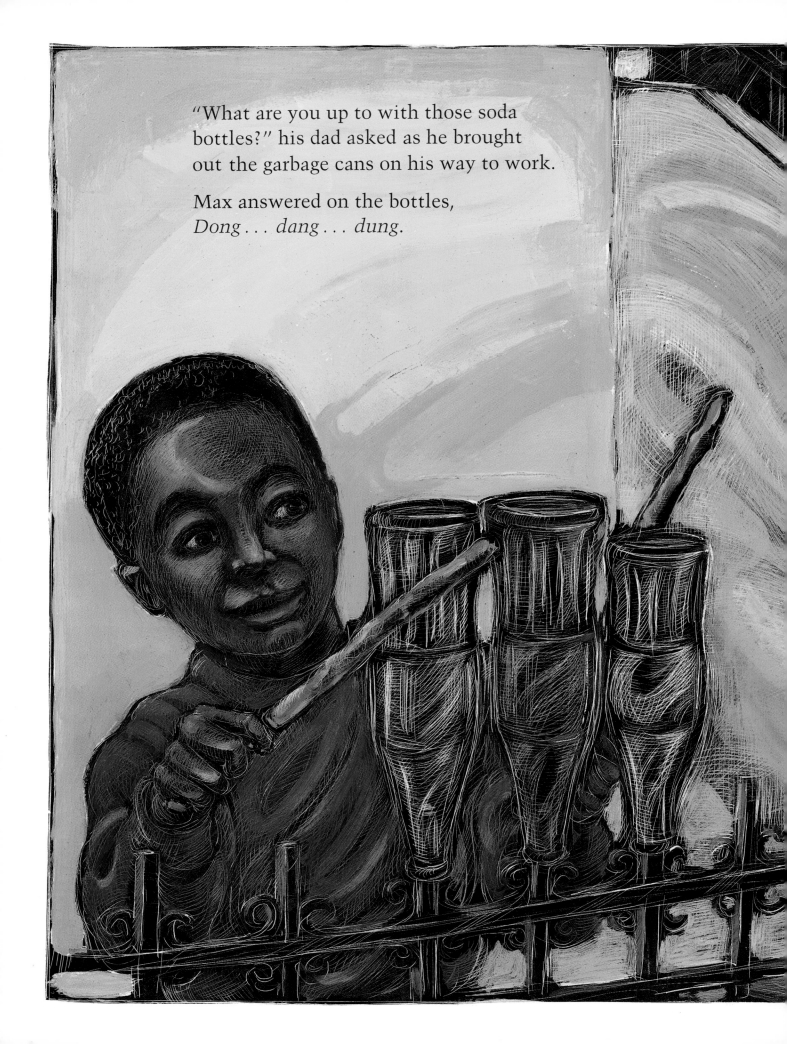

"What are you up to with those soda bottles?" his dad asked as he brought out the garbage cans on his way to work.

Max answered on the bottles,
Dong . . . dang . . . dung.

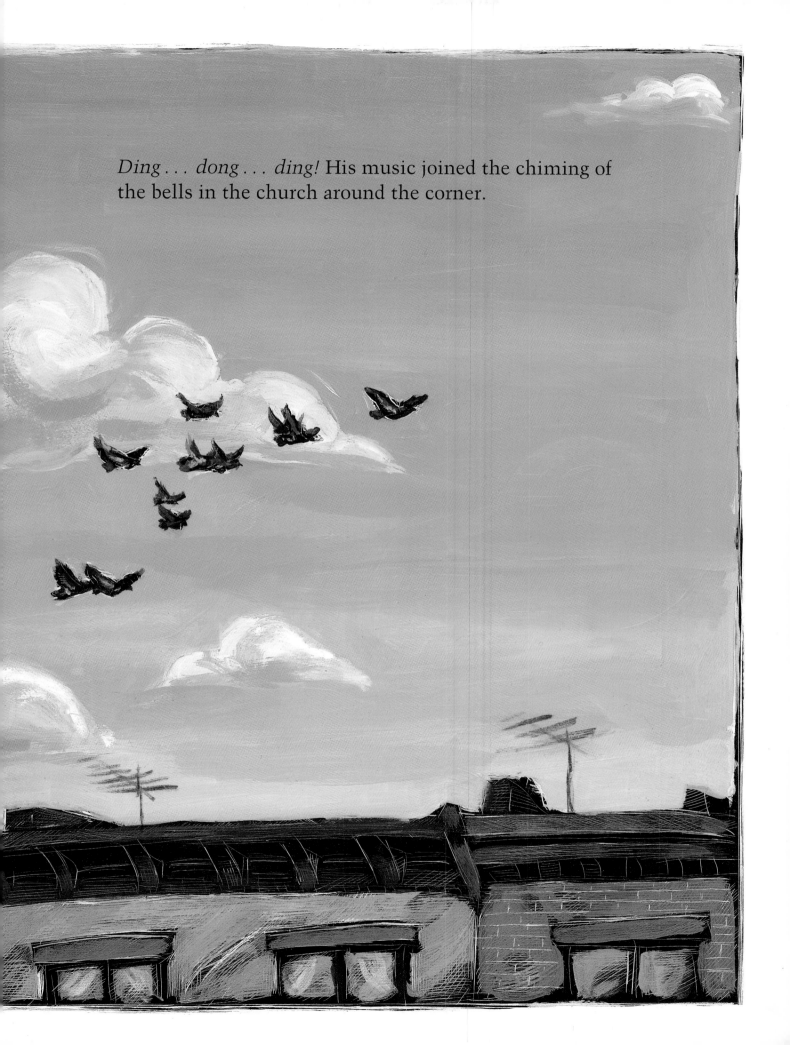

Ding . . . dong . . . ding! His music joined the chiming of the bells in the church around the corner.

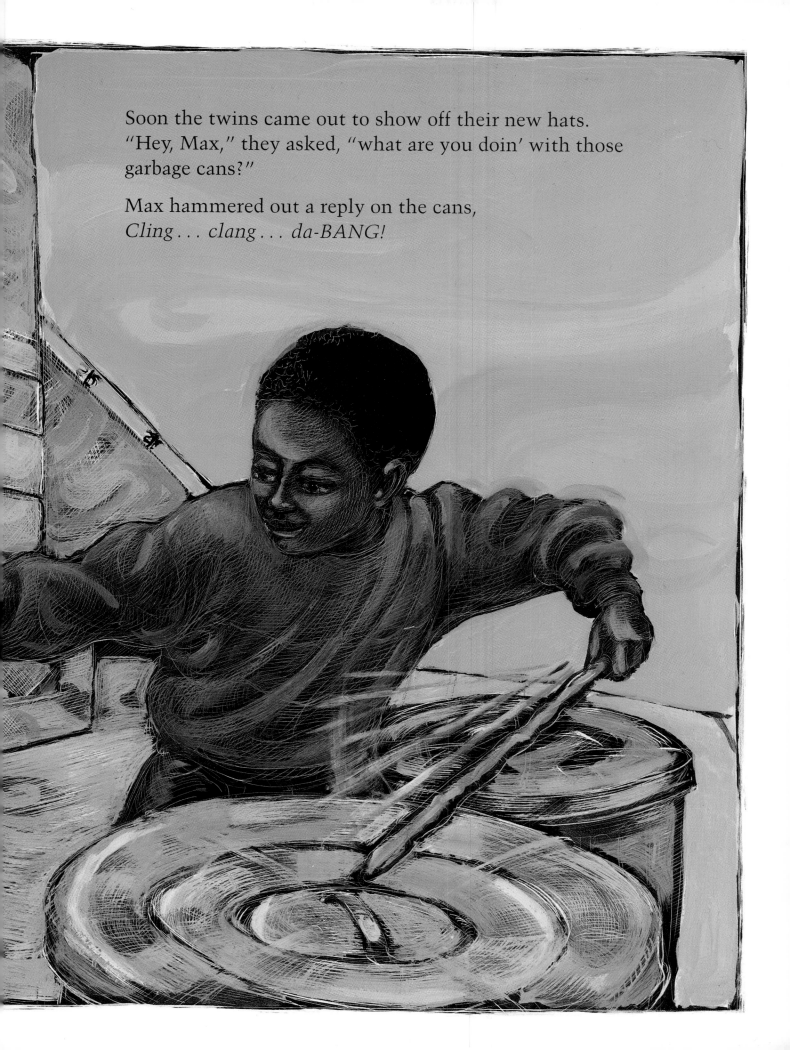

Soon the twins came out to show off their new hats.
"Hey, Max," they asked, "what are you doin' with those
garbage cans?"

Max hammered out a reply on the cans,
Cling . . . clang . . . da-BANG!

A-cling-clang . . . DA-BANGGGG!
Max pounded out the sound of the wheels thundering down the tracks under the train on which his father worked as a conductor.

Suddenly Max heard *Thump-di-di-thump* . . .
THUMP-DI-DI-THUMP! as a marching
band rounded the corner.

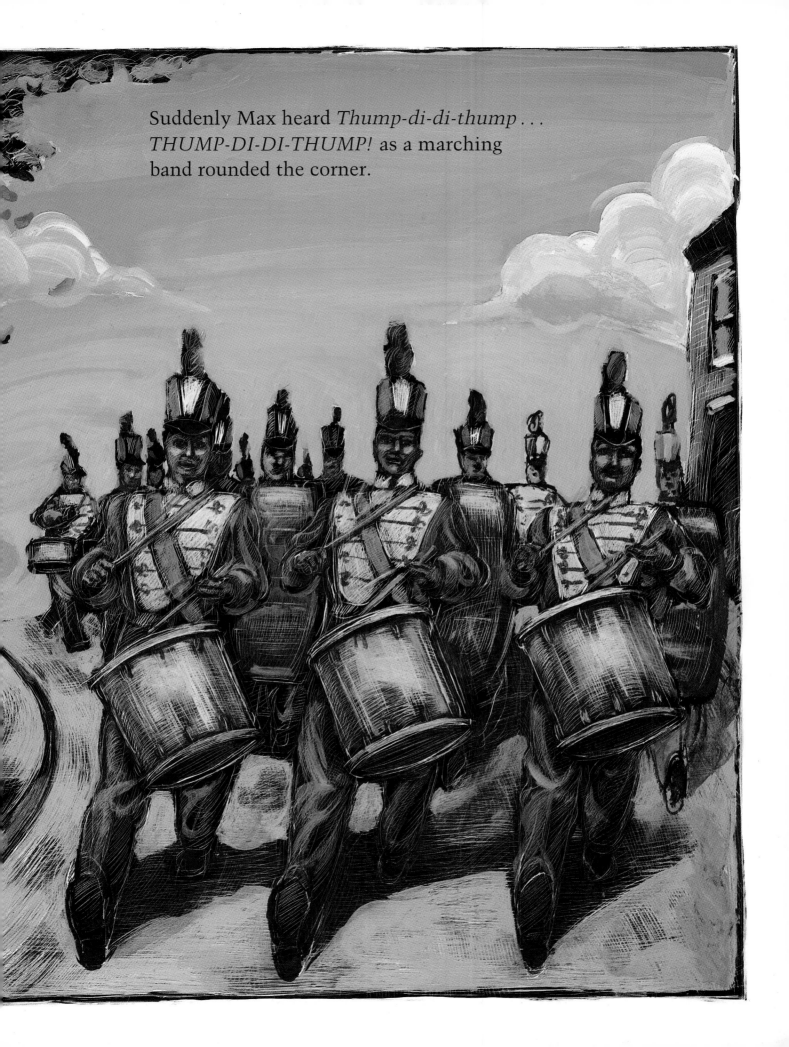

Max watched the drummers with amazement as they passed,
copying their rhythms. The last drummer saw Max.
Then with a nod and a wink, he tossed Max his spare
set of sticks.

"Thanks," called Max—and he didn't miss a beat.

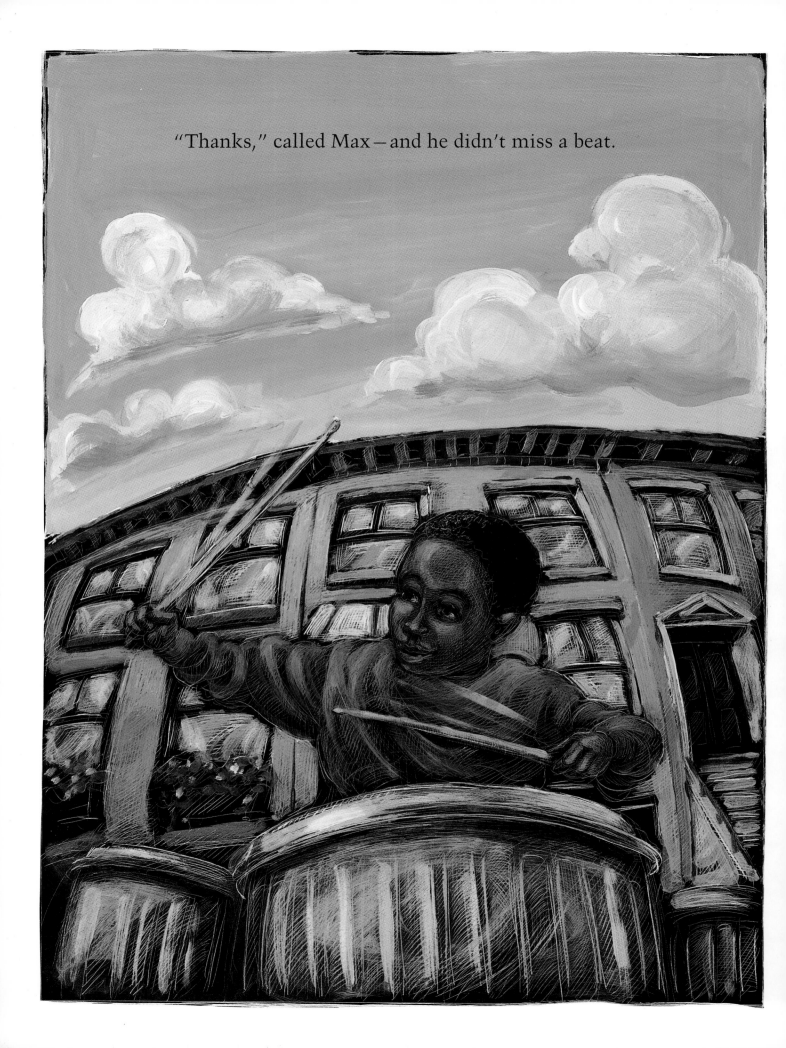

First Aladdin Paperbacks edition June 1997
Copyright © 1994 by Brian Pinkney

Aladdin Paperbacks
An imprint of Simon & Schuster
Children's Publishing Division
1230 Avenue of the Americas
New York, NY 10020

Designed by David Neuhaus
The text for this book was set in 14 point Trump Mediaeval.
The illustrations were done on scratchboard with oil paint and gouache.
Manufactured in China

16 18 20 19 17 15

The Library of Congress has cataloged the hardcover edition as follows:
Pinkney, J. Brian. Max Found Two Sticks / by Brian Pinkney.
p.   cm.
Summary: Although he doesn't feel like talking, a young boy responds
to questions by drumming on various objects, including a bucket, hat boxes,
and garbage cans.
[1. Drum—Fiction.   2. Afro-Americans—Fiction.]   I. Title.
PZ7.P63324Max   1994
[E]—dc20   93-12525
CIP
ISBN: 0-671-78776-4

ISBN: 0-689-81593-X (Aladdin pbk.)
ISBN-13: 978-0-689-81593-5 (Aladdin pbk.)